THE FABULOUS LOST & FOUND

AND THE LITTLE POLISH MOUSE

WRITTEN BY MARK PALLIS
ILLUSTRATED BY PETER BAYNTON

NEU WESTEND
— PRESS —

For Emily and Lucy. Legends! - MP

For Hannah and Skye - PB

THE FABULOUS LOST & FOUND AND THE LITTLE POLISH MOUSE
Copyright text © 2020 Mark Pallis and Copyright images © 2020 Peter Baynton

First Printing, 2020
ISBN: 978-1-9160801-3-3
NeuWestendPress.com

THE FABULOUS LOST & FOUND

AND THE LITTLE POLISH MOUSE

WRITTEN BY MARK PALLIS
ILLUSTRATED BY PETER BAYNTON

NEU WESTEND
— PRESS —

In the middle of the big city is a tiny
yellow building. If anyone loses anything, this is
where it ends up.

It is called the Lost and Found.

Mr and Mrs Frog keep everything safe, hoping that someday every lost watch and bag and phone and toy and shoe and cheesegrater will find its owner again.

But the shop is very small. And there are so many lost things. It is all quite a squeeze, but still, it's fabulous.

One sunny day, a little mouse walked in.

"Welcome," said Mrs Frog. "What have you lost?"

"Zgubiłam czapkę," said the mouse.

Mr and Mrs Frog could not speak Polish. They had no idea what the little mouse was saying.

What shall we do? they wondered.

Maybe she's lost an umbrella. Everyone loses an umbrella at least twice, thought Mr Frog.

"Have you lost this?" asked Mr Frog.

"Parasol? Nie," replied the mouse.

Then Mrs Frog remembered something that had been handed in a few months ago...

"Is this yours?" Mrs Frog asked, holding up a chunk of cheese.

"Ser? Nie. Smierdzi!" said the mouse.

"Time to put that cheese in the bin dear," said Mr Frog.

"Maybe the word 'czapka' means coat," said Mr Frog.

"Now where did I put that nice
yellow one?"

"Got it!" said Mr Frog.

"Płaszcz? Nie. Zgubiłam czapkę,"
said the mouse.

She was starting to feel a bit frustrated.

"We need to keep trying," said Mrs Frog.

Nie szalik.

Nie spodnie.

Nie sweter.

Nie buty.

Nie okulary
przeciwsłoneczne.

"Zgubiłam czapkę," said the
mouse.

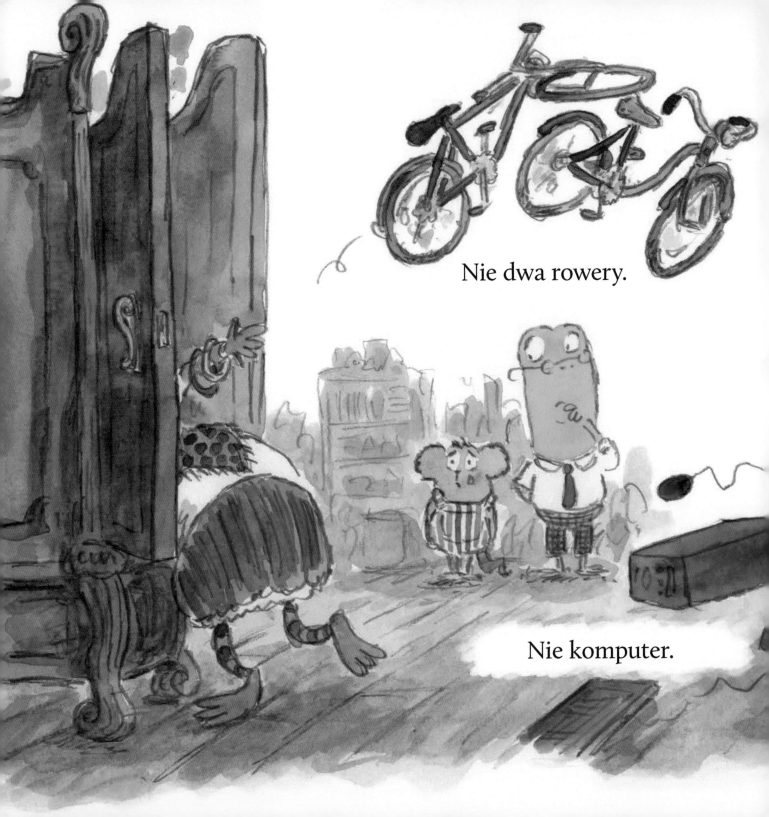

Nie dwa rowery.

Nie komputer.

Nie trzy książki.

Nie cztery banany.

Nie pięć kluczy.

It was no good. A fat wet tear rolled down the mouse's cheek.

"How about a nice cup of tea?" asked Mrs Frog kindly.

"Uwielbiam herbatę. Dzięki," replied the mouse. They sat together, sipping their tea and all feeling a bit sad.

Suddenly, the mouse realised she could try pointing.

She pointed at her head.
"Czapka," she said.

"I've got it!" exclaimed Mrs Frog, leaping up.

"A wig of course!" said Mrs Frog.

"Nie peruka," said the mouse.

Nie czerwona.

Nie blond.

Nie brązowa.

Nie kolorowa.

Nie zielona.

"What about this?"
asked Mr Frog, pulling back
a curtain.

"Tak!" exclaimed the
mouse.

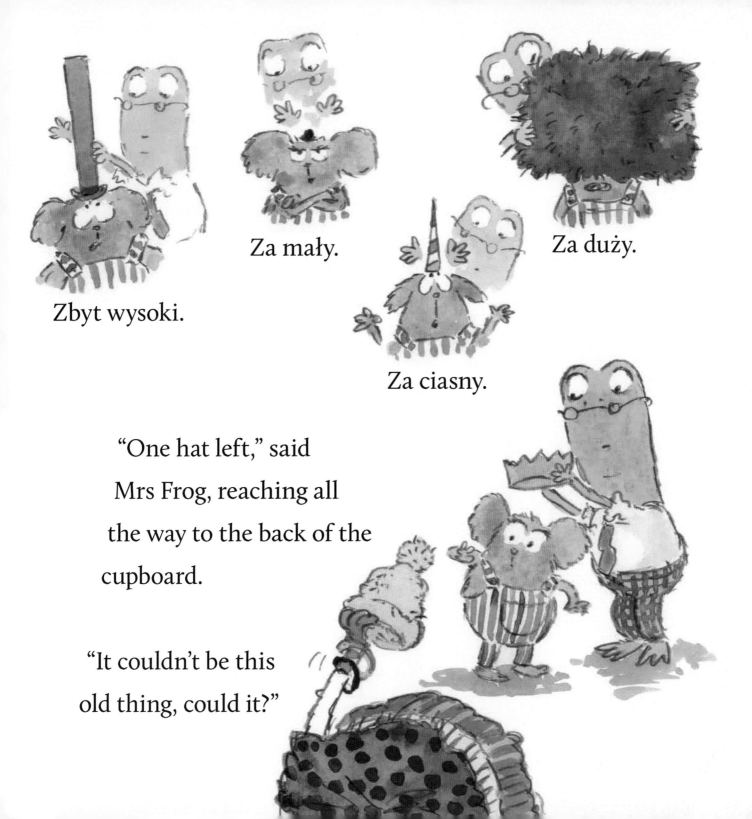

Zbyt wysoki.

Za mały.

Za ciasny.

Za duży.

"One hat left," said
Mrs Frog, reaching all
the way to the back of the
cupboard.

"It couldn't be this
old thing, could it?"

"Moja czapka. Znalazłam swoją czapkę!

Dziękuję bardzo," said the mouse.

"Ah, so 'czapka' means hat. Wonderful,"

smiled Mr and Mrs Frog.

And just like that, the mouse found her hat.

"Do widzenia," she said, as she skipped away.
"Do widzenia," replied Mr and Mrs Frog.

"I wonder who will come tomorrow?" said Mr Frog.
Mrs Frog put her arm around him.

"I don't know," she replied, giving him a squeeze,
"but whoever it is, we'll do our best to help."

LEARNING TO LOVE LANGUAGES

An additional language opens a child's mind, broadens their horizons and enriches their emotional life. Research has shown that the time between a child's birth and their sixth or seventh birthday is a "golden period" when they are most receptive to new languages. This is because they have an in-built ability to distinguish the sounds they hear and make sense of them. The Story-powered Language Learning Method taps into these natural abilities.

HOW THE STORY-POWERED LANGUAGE LEARNING METHOD WORKS

We create an emotionally engaging and funny story for children and adults to enjoy together, just like any other picture book. Studies show that social interaction, like enjoying a book together, is critical in language learning.

Through the story, we introduce a relatable character who speaks only in the new language. This helps build empathy and a positive attitude towards people who speak different languages. These are both important aspects in laying the foundations for lasting language acquisition in a child's life.

As the story progresses, the child naturally works with the characters to discover the meanings of a wide range of fun new words. Strategic use of humour ensures that this subconscious learning is rewarded with laughter; the child feels good and the first seeds of a lifelong love of languages are sown.

For more information and free downloads visit www.neuwestendpress.com

ALL THE BEAUTIFUL POLISH WORDS AND PHRASES FROM OUR STORY

zgubiłam czapkę	I've lost my hat
parasol	umbrella
ser	cheese
śmierdzi	stinks
płaszcz	coat
szalik	scarf
spodnie	trousers
okulary przeciwsłoneczne	sunglasses
sweter	sweater
buty	shoes
jeden	one
dwa	two
trzy	three
cztery	four
pięć	five
komputer	computer
książki	books
kluczy	keys
rowery	bicycles
banany	bananas
uwielbiam herbatę	I love tea
dzięki	thanks
peruka	wig
czerwona	red (f)
blond	blond
brązowa	brown (f)
zielona	green (f)
kolorowa	multicoloured (f)

nie	no
moja czapka	my hat
zbyt wysoki	too tall
za duży	too big
za mały	too small
za ciasny	too tight
znalazłam swoją czapkę	I've found my hat
dziękuję bardzo	thank you very much
do widzenia	goodbye

THE WORLD OF
THE FABULOUS LOST & FOUND

THIS STORY IS ALSO AVAILABLE IN...

FRENCH   SPANISH

ITALIAN   CZECH

KOREAN   WELSH

GERMAN   HEBREW

SWEDISH   GREEK   SLOVAKIAN

VIETNAMESE   LATIN   PORTUGUESE

...AND MANY MORE LANGUAGES!

ENJOYED IT?
WRITE A REVIEW AND
LET US KNOW!

@MARK_PALLIS ON TWITTER
WWW.MARKPALLIS.COM

@PETERBAYNTON ON INSTAGRAM
WWW.PETERBAYNTON.COM